D0479369

For Dad—you always have time for silly stories. And Grandma Pat & Uncle Gene, for taking in a refugee family and calling us your own. —D.D.

For Faraday and Ricky. And my mom—who always inspired me to create. —H.R.

WHEN TO WASH YOUR HANDS:

- If they're dirty
- Before eating or touching food
- After going to the ~~bathroom~~
- ~~After~~ playing with pets
- After sneezing, coughing, blowing your nose or being around someone ~~sick~~

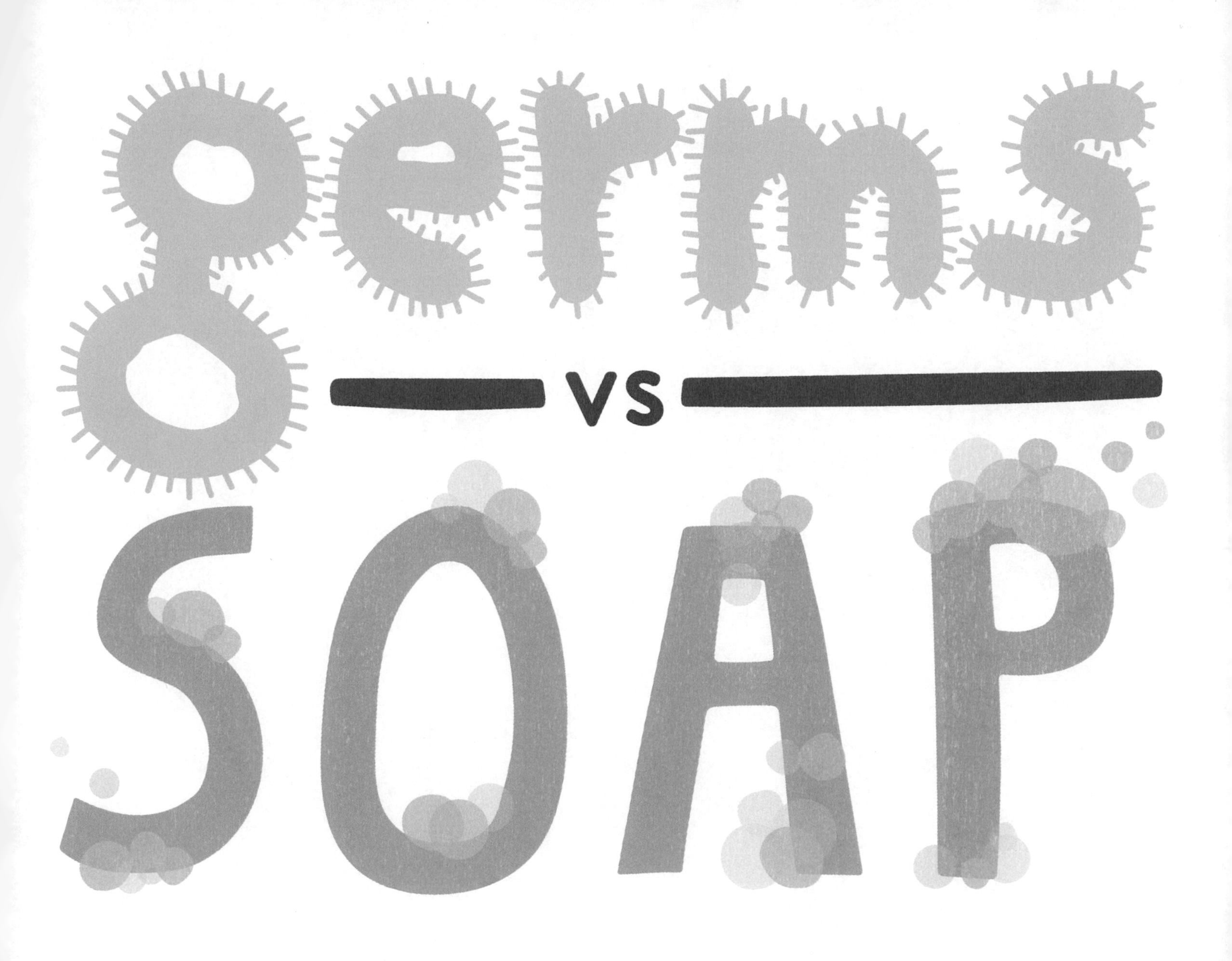

Written by

Didi Dragon

Illustrated by

Hannah Robinett

Once upon a time, and maybe even right at this moment, there were germs on hands.

Of course, germs are so tiny you can't see them with your eyes, but that doesn't mean they're too tiny to dream of energy cupcakes all day.

There is, however, one thing that crushes a germ's sweet cupcake dream—

Soap. Germs absolutely, positively, do NOT like soap.

At germ school, germs learn how to be germy. The teacher asks questions like, "Why are hands the very best place for germs to be?"

That's right. Eyes, noses and mouths are like open doors for germs. And once they get in, it's time for energy cupcakes—

ENERGY CUPCAKES!

You're probably thinking, what are energy cupcakes?
Well, they're not *real* cupcakes.
You see, germs survive in our bodies by gobbling up our energy.
And when hungry germs see energy, it looks like cupcakes—energy cupcakes!

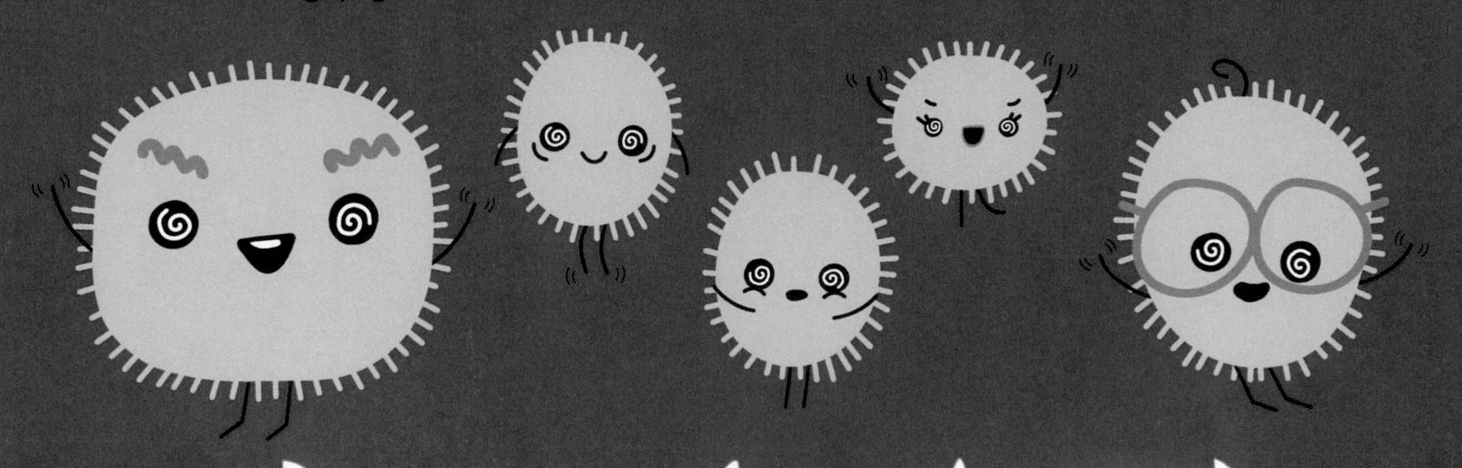

ENERGY CUPCAKES!

Once the germs finally settle down,
they reflect on the importance
of being on hands.

All germs know that eating lots of energy cupcakes—

—makes them toot. A lot.

The toot could be a silent toot, a medium toot, or even a loud trumpet toot—germs don't care. They just have to be stinky.

Because stinky toots get kids sick.

A sick kid will start sneezing and coughing, so that the germs just fly outta there onto someone new. And you know what that means?
More energy cupcakes.

Unless the germs find themselves right in front of the sink (probably because an adult told the kid to go wash their hands).

Luckily for the germs, there's no more soap in the bathroom.
Maybe the kid will just wash their hands with water?

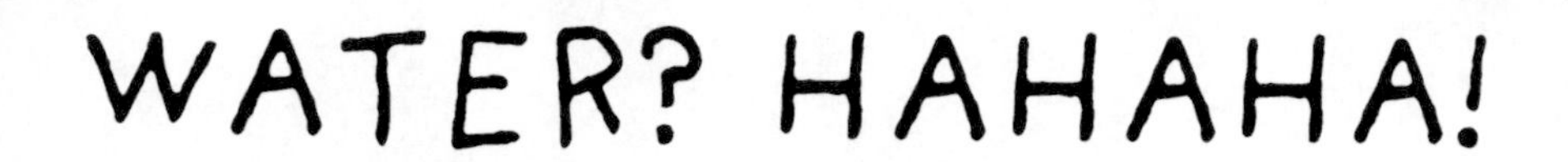

It's quite a celebration for the germs, you know,
if there's no more soap in the bathroom.
In fact, it's officially called a no-soap party.

All parties must come to an end, especially when an adult is sniffing for the soap smell.
Uh-oh. It's the adult's nose right above us! Code 931, code 931, code 931!
Nooooooooo! Wait, what's that mean again?
Oh, for Pete's sake! Code 931 is the sniff-test, Arnold! It means we're going to get washed!

But the germs don't give up that easily.
They remind themselves that they've been here for bazillions and bazillions of years. They've outlived the dinosaurs, for crying out loud!

It's always a good idea to double-check before making any sudden moves.

AHHHHHH!!!!!

Germs know to rush to the safe zones. Well, some of them.

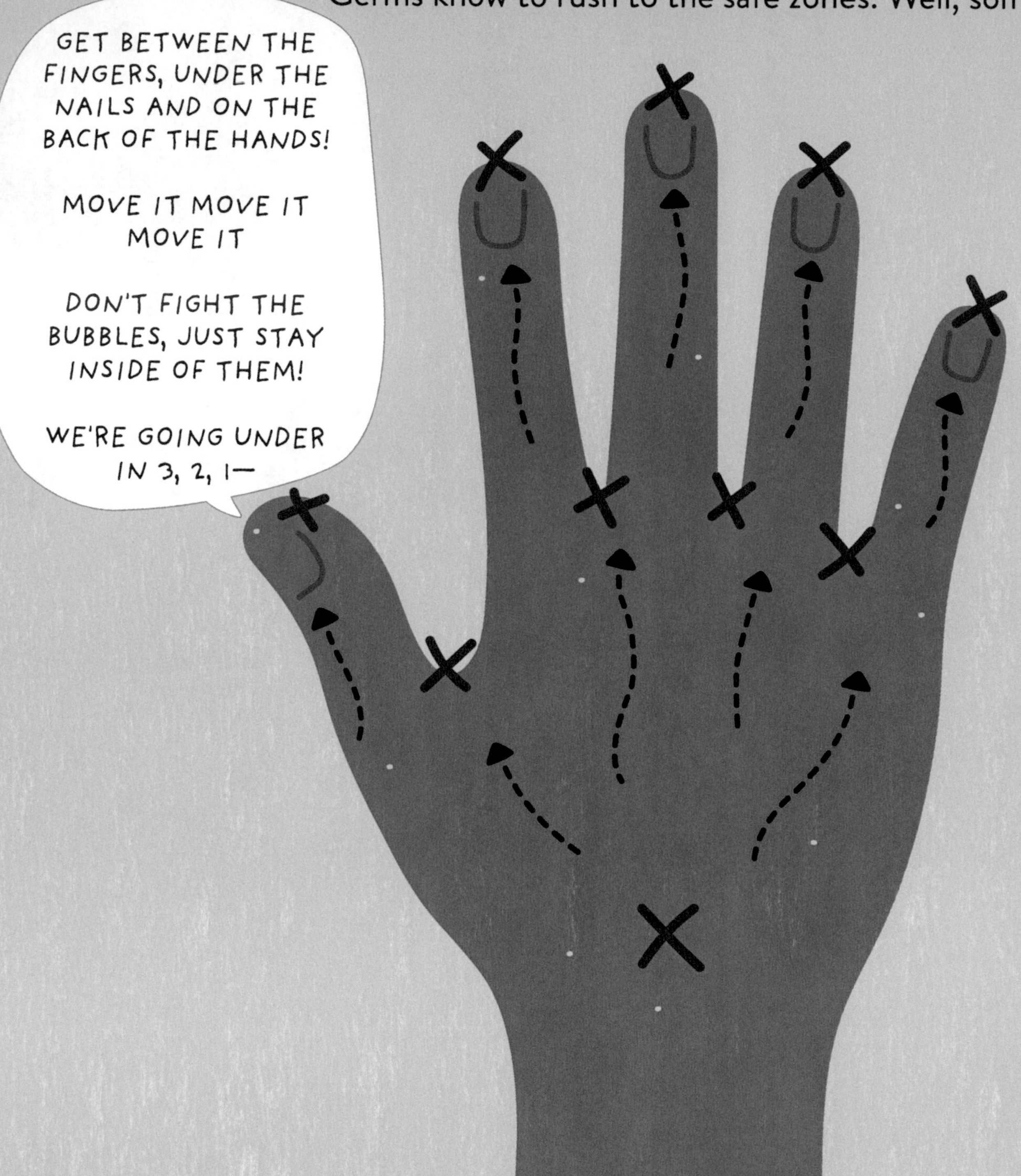

Arnold, get away from the middle of the palm! You're gonna get—
jerns were here
Ewww, this soap is so cold and slimy!
Whoa, it's way too slippery here. I can't even hang on anymore!
Hey, you know what? This soap isn't too bad—blach, blech, gag, gaaaaa!

The germs prepare to get scrubbed . . . for at least 20 seconds:

Rub hands, palm to palm

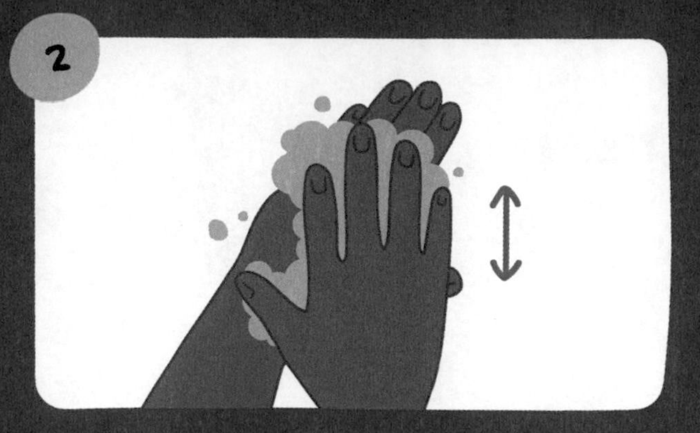

Back of hands, too

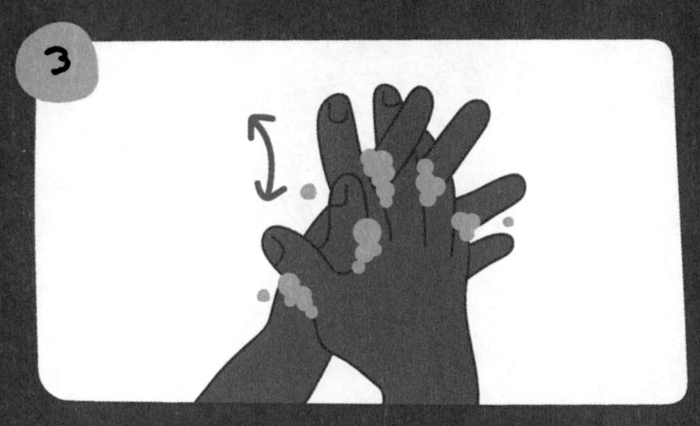

In between fingers

Back of fingers

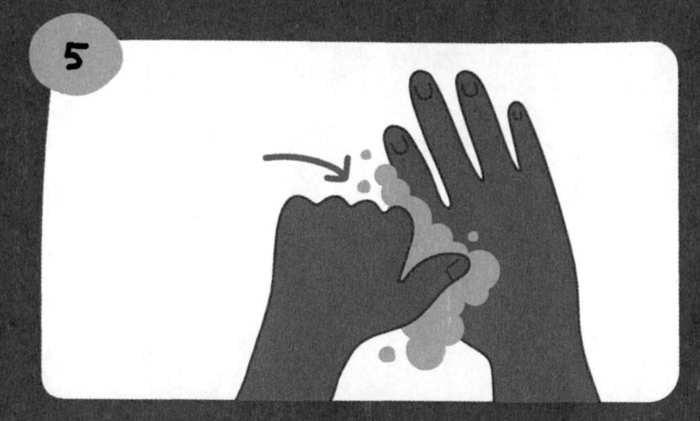

Don't forget about thumbs

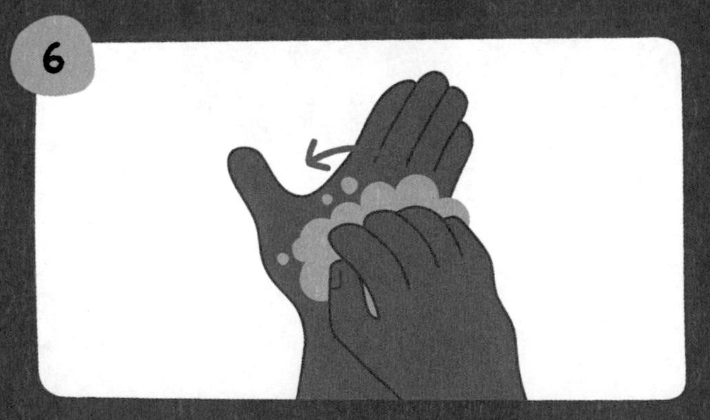

And under nails

In all that commotion, the germs get distracted by the bubbles.

But none of them could have prepared for this moment:

GUYS, WATCH OUT!

It proves to be a little fun for some of them.
Hey look! He's on a bubble!
What up, dudes and dudettes! Don't mind me, just surfing down the line!
Soap fumes.
What's wrong with him?
Brah, is that a shark?
Uh, you know we're not really in the ocean, right?

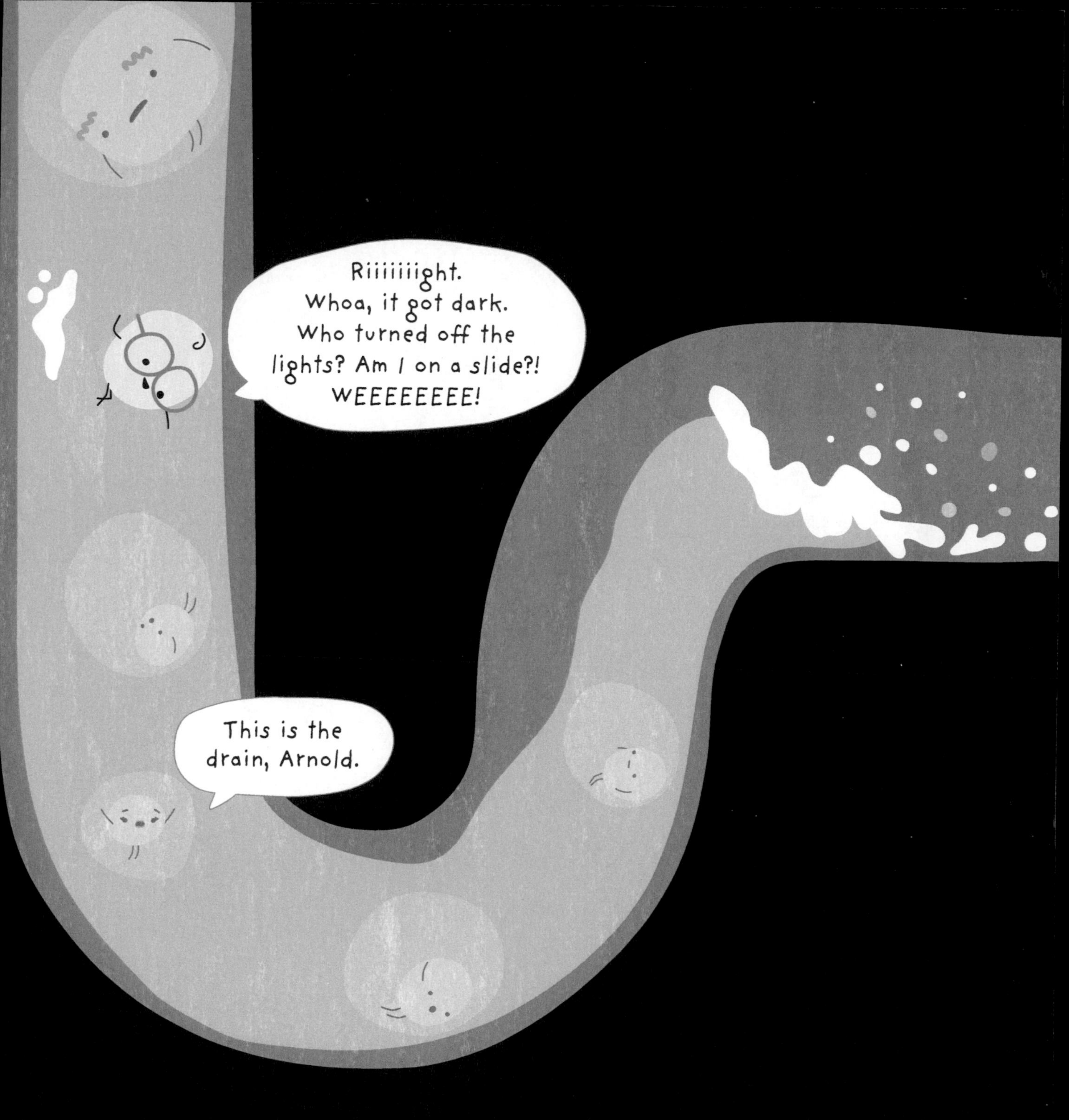
Riiiiiiiight.
Whoa, it got dark.
Who turned off the
lights? Am I on a slide?!
WEEEEEEEE!
This is the
drain, Arnold.

Ohhhh, look! It's an energy cupcake. Yummy!
That's old toothpaste, Arnold!

And so the germs go down the drain.

THE END.

And there'll be
more soap.

This book was rejected 43 times, so it's independently published by AHA! Press.
Get out there and write your own books.

Environmental consciousness is important. This book is printed on acid-free paper supplied by a Forest Stewardship Council-certified provider. The ink is chlorine-free.

First Edition

Library of Congress Cataloging-in-Publication Data on file.

ISBN 978-1-7352524-0-7

Sorry to disappoint, but **Didi Dragon** is not actually a dragon. She has one dragon-like tendency, though, which is she can only sleep in cold, dark rooms, kinda like a cave. Otherwise she's rather jumpy with sudden noises, and hiccups if her tacos are too spicy. If she could have a super power, it would be to fly, of course. She likes to roller skate, dance while cleaning, and play futbol. She's not very good at those things, but it sure looks like she has fun.

Oh yeah, she's currently writing *Cavities vs. Toothpaste*. You can visit her at didivsdragon.com.

Hannah Robinett grew up drawing plants and landscapes during boring summer jobs. After moving to NYC to pursue her art for real, she took quite the turn and fell in love with the process of conceptual art. Now she is a full-time artist, and you can find her cutting up her work and drawing pixel-perfect grids. When she's not at her studio, she is probably knee-deep in craft supplies with her daughter or creating intricate food plates for her family. Hannah lives in the beautiful borough of Brooklyn with her daughter Faraday, husband Ricky, and silly pomeranian, Gif. The moral of her story is: don't wait for the perfect moment. Always be creating!

HELLO
MY NAME IS...
DAX
I'M FROM:
DOOR KNOB

HELLO
MY NAME IS...
Arnold
I'M FROM:
toilet